Lyndon B. Johnson

BY DIANE MARCZELY GIMPEL

The Child's World®
childsworld.com

Published by The Child's World®
1980 Lookout Drive • Mankato, MN 56003-1705
800-599-READ • www.childsworld.com

Acknowledgments
The Child's World®: Mary Swensen, Publishing Director
Red Line Editorial: Editorial direction and production
The Design Lab: Design

Photographs ©: Arnold Newman/LBJ Library photo, cover, 1;
Cecil Stoughton/White House/John F. Kennedy Presidential
Library and Museum, Boston, 4; Cecil Stoughton/LBJ
Library photo, 7; Corbis, 8; Austin American-Statesman/LBJ
Library photo, 11; Bettmann/Corbis, 12; John Vachon/FSA/
OWI Collection/Library of Congress, 14; Robert Knudsen/
LBJ Library photo, 17; Frank Wolfe/LBJ Library photo, 18;
Bob Daemmrich/Corbis, 21

ISBN 9781503808706
LCCN 2015958434

Printed in the United States of America
Mankato, MN
June, 2016
PA02303

ABOUT THE AUTHOR

Diane Marczely Gimpel is a former newspaper reporter, an author, and a social studies and English teacher. She lives near Philadelphia with her husband and two sons.

Table of Contents

★ ★ ★

Kennedy and Johnson rode through Dallas, Texas, the day Kennedy was killed.

CHAPTER ONE

A Tragic Beginning

Lyndon B. Johnson visited Texas on November 22, 1963. Texas was where he grew up. Now, he was vice president of the United States. The trip was important. Some Texans did not like President John F. Kennedy. Kennedy wanted more Texans to like him. He thought visiting the state with Johnson might help. Texans liked Johnson.

The two men rode through Dallas, Texas. Johnson was two cars behind the president. People looked happy to see Kennedy. They waved and cheered. Then, a gun fired. The noise surprised Johnson. A

Secret Service agent pushed him to the floor of the car. The Secret Service protects the president and vice president. Johnson was not hurt. But the bullets hit Kennedy. Their cars raced to the hospital. Johnson waited there. Doctors tried to save Kennedy's life. Then, one of Kennedy's best friends came to talk to Johnson. The friend said Kennedy had died.

Johnson became president about two hours later. He said he would be a good president. He would **defend** America's laws. Then, he left for Washington, DC. He talked to reporters there. He said he knew Kennedy's death made people sad. He was sad, too. But he would do his best. He asked for everyone to help him. He became the 36th president of the United States.

Johnson took the oath of office on an airplane.

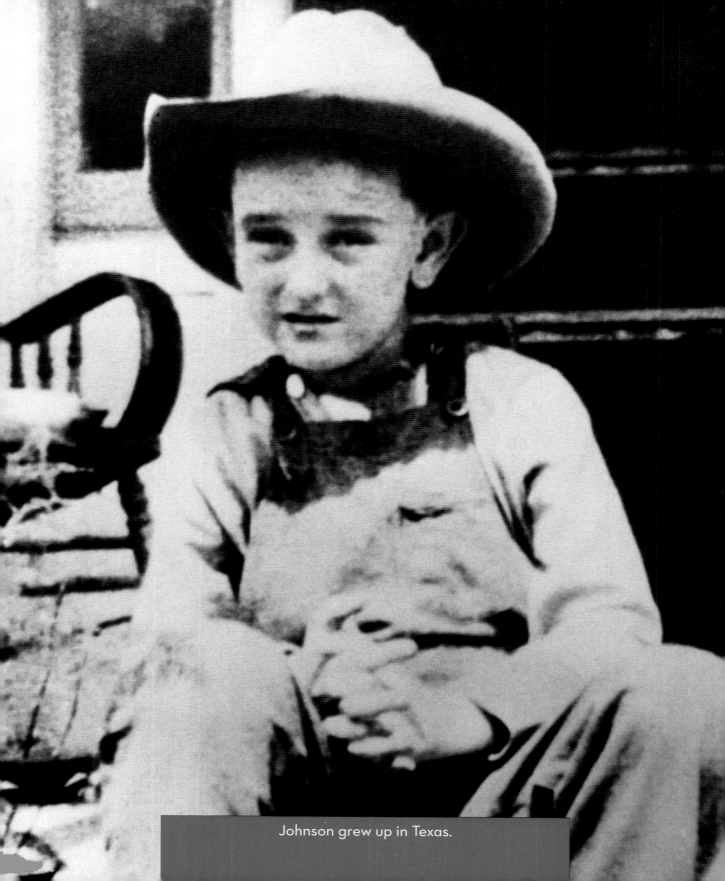

Johnson grew up in Texas.

CHAPTER TWO

The Making of a President

Johnson was born August 27, 1908, in Stonewall, Texas. He was poor. He graduated from high school when he was 15. Then, he started working. He ran an elevator. He made it stop and go. He then helped build roads. In 1927, he started college. And he kept working. He cleaned buildings. He helped in an office. He taught at a school. His students were Mexican American children. Many were very poor. Johnson saw how **poverty** hurt them. Their school had few teachers. It had no money for lunches or sports equipment. Most students did not go on to college. They could not afford it. Other people did not treat them well. He wanted to help these students.

Johnson graduated from college in 1930. He kept teaching. Then, he went to Washington, DC. He worked for a man in Congress. Congress makes laws. On a visit home, he met Claudia Alta Taylor. Her nickname was Lady Bird. They married on November 17, 1934. He took a job in Texas. He helped young people find work.

Johnson was **elected** to the U.S. House of Representatives in 1937. That is a part of Congress. He worked to get electricity to farms. He tried to stop the government from wasting money. Johnson signed up to fight in World War II. He was the first person in Congress to sign up. He fought from 1941 to 1942.

Johnson met Lady Bird in 1934.

Johnson (left) worked hard in the Senate.

He won a Silver Star award for bravery. Then, he returned to Congress. In 1948, Johnson was elected to the U.S. Senate. He was part of a political **party** called the Democratic Party. People in that party had been disagreeing with each other. But Johnson worked hard. He won their support. He united them. Unity helped pass laws. The Civil Rights Act of 1957 protected Americans' right to vote. Some white people in the early 1900s did not treat African Americans fairly. Some white people kept them from voting. The Civil Rights Act meant the government could stop people who kept others from voting.

Johnson was powerful. He hoped he could be president. But the Democrats chose John F. Kennedy. Kennedy asked Johnson to be vice president. Johnson agreed. They won. But Kennedy was killed in 1963. Johnson became president.

COLORED WAITING ROOM

African Americans were separated from white people in many places such as railroad stations.

CHAPTER THREE

Johnson as President

Johnson did what Kennedy had wanted. Johnson lowered **taxes**. He signed the Civil Rights Act of 1964. At that time, African Americans were treated unfairly. African Americans were often separated from white people. White people could refuse to hire an African American because of skin color. With this act, there could be no separation in public places. Companies could not refuse to hire someone because of skin color.

Johnson ran for president in 1964. He won. He wanted to make a "Great **Society**." He wanted everyone to be equal. He wanted to get rid of poverty. So he created Medicare and Medicaid. They help the **elderly** and poor get health care. He helped poor students go to school.

Johnson's work was hard. There were big challenges. The Vietnam War started in 1964. Johnson tried to stop **communists** from taking over South Vietnam. He sent many soldiers to fight.

At the same time, Johnson signed an important law. It was the Voting Rights Act of 1965. African Americans were still being denied the right to vote. This law made that illegal. Johnson thought it was the best thing he did. He signed the law in the President's Room. That room was special. President Abraham Lincoln signed a law there in 1861. It freed **slaves** who had fought in the Civil War.

Johnson signed the Voting Rights Act of 1965.

But Americans liked Johnson less and less. Many did not like the Vietnam War. It cost a lot of money. And by 1968, more than half a million Americans were fighting in Vietnam. Thousands had died. Many more had been hurt. The war seemed to drag on. Some people grew angry.

Johnson did not run for president again. Most Americans did not like his choices in the war. He left the White House in 1969. He wanted to focus on peace in America and Vietnam.

Johnson lived at his Texas ranch after his presidency.

CHAPTER FOUR

Life after the Presidency

Johnson moved back to Texas. He owned a ranch near his hometown. He had animals and land. He worked on his ranch. He played golf. He wrote a book about being president.

Johnson got weekly news from the White House. President Richard Nixon sent it to Johnson's ranch by plane. Sometimes people who worked for Nixon came, too. They talked to Johnson about the Vietnam War's progress.

But Johnson was not in great health. He had a heart attack on January 22, 1973. He died in his home. The war had not ended yet. He never saw peace in Vietnam. He was buried on his ranch. His wife lived there until she died in 2007. Then, Johnson's ranch became a park. Visitors can go there to learn about his life.

People have different opinions about Lyndon B. Johnson. The Vietnam War made some people upset. But Johnson also helped America. He made health care more available. He worked to protect Americans' rights. His work changed America.

Visitors enjoy a yearly barbecue at Johnson's ranch.

1900

← **August 27, 1908** Lyndon B. Johnson is born in Texas.

← **August 19, 1930** Johnson graduates from Southwest Texas State Teachers College.

← **November 17, 1934** Johnson marries Claudia Alta "Lady Bird" Taylor.

← **April 10, 1937** Johnson is elected to the U.S. House of Representatives.

← **November 2, 1948** Johnson is elected to the U.S. Senate.

← **July 14, 1960** Johnson becomes a candidate for vice president of the United States.

← **November 8, 1960** John F. Kennedy and Johnson win the presidential election.

← **January 20, 1961** Kennedy and Johnson begin their jobs as president and vice president.

← **November 22, 1963** Kennedy is killed in Texas. Johnson becomes president.

← **November 3, 1964** Johnson is elected president.

← **March 31, 1968** Johnson announces he will not seek reelection.

← **January 20, 1969** Johnson retires to his ranch in Texas.

← **January 22, 1973** Johnson dies of a heart attack at his ranch.

1980

communists (KOM-yoo-nists) Communists are people who believe the government should own everything and give everything to the people equally. Communists tried to control Vietnam.

defend (di-FEND) To defend something is to protect it. Johnson promised to defend America's laws.

elderly (EL-dur-lee) A person who is elderly is old. Johnson helped the elderly get health care.

elected (ih-LEK-tid) Someone who is elected is chosen by a vote. Johnson was elected to the U.S. Senate.

party (PAHR-tee) A party is a group made up of voters with the same ideas and goals for the government. Johnson belonged to the Democratic Party.

poverty (PAWV-ur-tee) Poverty exists when people have very little money and own very little. People who are poor live in poverty.

slaves (SLAVES) Slaves are people who are owned and controlled by other people. Abraham Lincoln freed the slaves.

society (suh-SYE-uh-tee) A society is everyone who lives in a country or area. Johnson wanted America to be a "Great Society."

taxes (TAKS-es) Taxes are money that people and companies pay the government. Johnson wanted to lower taxes so people would pay less money to the government.

In the Library

Maupin, Melissa. *Lyndon Baines Johnson.*
Mankato, MN: The Child's World, 2009.

Venezia, Mike. *Lyndon B. Johnson: Thirty-Sixth President,
1963–1969.* New York: Children's Press, 2007.

Zullo, Allan. *Vietnam War: Heroes.* New York: Scholastic Inc., 2014.

On the Web

Visit our Web site for links about
Lyndon B. Johnson: **childsworld.com/links**

*Note to Parents, Teachers, and Librarians: We routinely verify our Web links to make
sure they are safe and active sites. So encourage your readers to check them out!*

INDEX